A Giant First-Start® Reader

This easy reader contains only 47 words,
repeated often to help the young reader develop
word recognition and interest in reading.

Basic word list for *Bubble Trouble Ghost*

a	gum	over
all	Gus	pop
and	has	red
at	he	round
blows	I	says
blue	in	stop
bubble	is	that
chew	it	the
chews	like	this
chewy	look	treat
does	lots	trick
end	no	trouble
ghost	now	what
goodies	of	yes
gooey	or	you
green	orange	

Bubble Trouble Ghost

by Janet Craig

illustrated by Patrick Girouard

Troll Associates

Look at Gus.

Gus has goodies.

He has lots and lots of trick-or-treat goodies.

What is this?
A trick or a treat?

It is round.
It is blue.

Pop it in.
Chew and chew.

Bubble gum!

Gooey, chewy bubble gum!
"I like gum," says Gus.
Gus chews and chews.

He blows and blows . . .

and blows
and blows . . .

"Stop, Gus! Stop!"
POP!

Now *that* is bubble trouble.

Does that stop Gus?

No.

What is this?

A trick or a treat?
It is round.
It is red.
Pop it in.
Chew and chew.

Bubble gum!
Gooey, chewy bubble gum!

"I like gum," says Gus.

Gus chews and chews.
He blows and blows . . .
and blows and blows . . .
POP!

"Stop, Gus! Stop!"
Now *that* is bubble trouble.

Does that stop Gus?
"I like gum," says Gus.
Red gum, green gum,
orange gum, blue.
Pop it in.
Chew, chew, chew!

Gus chews and chews.

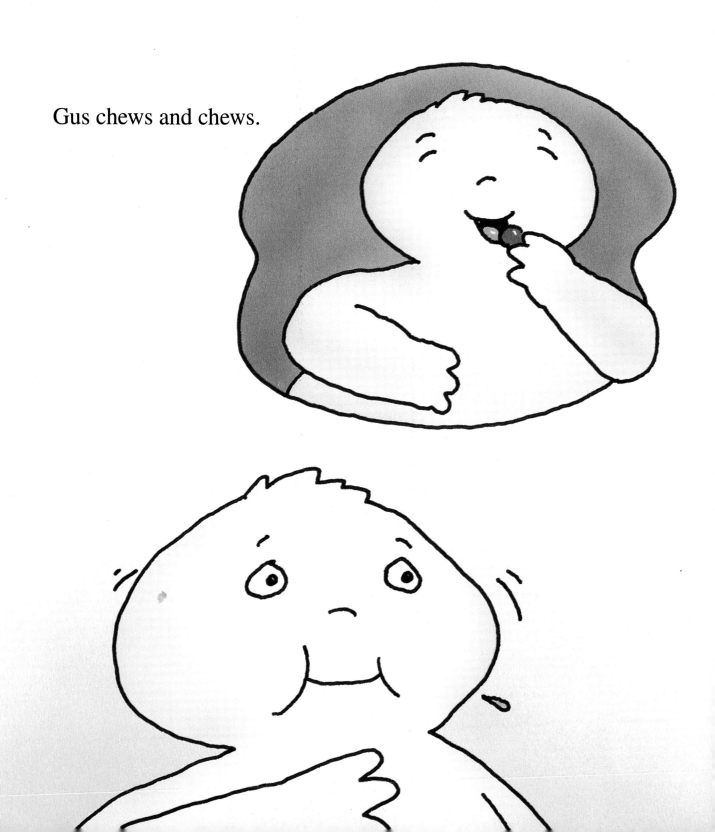

He blows and blows . . .
and blows and blows . . .

Look at you now, Gus.

Red gum, green gum,
orange gum, blue.

Gooey, chewy bubble gum
all over you!

Does that stop Gus?

Yes!

And *that* is the end of bubble trouble.